Acting the Story

Since then I've acted out *The Snail and the Whale* lots of times in schools and at festivals. At first, I had a big inflatable whale that I used to perform the story. It was easy enough to blow up but I had to sit on it, or even trample on it, to get all the air out again afterwards. Poor whale, being trampled on!

I had lots of little foam snails, with Velcro stuck on their bottoms so I could stick them onto a piece of black cloth that I used to drape over a chair as the rock. But how would the main snail write on the blackboard? Well, one of the snails was very special. It had a piece of chalk hidden inside it that I could use to write with. I just had to make sure that special snail never got left at home!

And now it's 15 years since the snail and her friend the whale first set sail, which is a great adventure indeed. And I wish them both a very Happy Birthday.

Julia Donaldson

WRITTEN BY

JULIA DONALDSON

ILLUSTRATED BY

AXEL SCHEFFLER

The Snail and the Whale

MACMILLAN CHILDREN'S BOOKS

This is a tale of a tiny snail

And a great big, grey-blue humpback whale.

This is a rock as black as soot,

And this is a snail with an itchy foot.

The sea snail slithered all over the rock

And gazed at the sea and the ships in the dock.

And as she gazed she sniffed and sighed.

"The sea is deep and the world is wide!

How I long to sail!"

Said the tiny snail.

These are the other snails in the flock,

Who all stuck tight to the smooth black rock

And said to the snail with the itchy foot,

"Be quiet! Don't wriggle! Sit still! Stay put!"

But the tiny sea snail sighed and sniffed,

Then cried, "I've got it! I'll hitch a lift!"

This is the trail

Of the tiny snail,

A silvery trail that looped and curled

And said . . .

This is the whale who came one night

When the tide was high and the stars were bright.

A humpback whale, immensely long,

Who sang to the snail a wonderful song

Of shimmering ice and coral caves

And shooting stars and enormous waves.

And this is the tail

Of the humpback whale.

He held it out of the starlit sea

And said to the snail,

"Come sail with me."

This is the sea,

So wild and free,

That carried the whale

And the snail on his tail

To towering icebergs and far-off lands,

With fiery mountains and golden sands.

These are the waves that arched and crashed,

That foamed and frolicked and sprayed

    and splashed

The tiny snail

On the tail of the whale.

These are the caves
Beneath the waves,
Where stripy fish with feathery fins
And sharks with hideous toothy grins
Swam round the whale
And the snail on his tail.

This is the sky

So vast and high,

Sometimes sunny and blue and warm,

Sometimes filled with a thunderstorm,

With zigzag lightning

Flashing and frightening

The tiny snail

On the tail of the whale.

And she gazed at the sky, the sea, the land,

The waves and the caves and the golden sand,

She gazed and gazed, amazed by it all,

And she said to the whale, "I feel so small."

But then came the day

The whale lost his way . . .

These are the speedboats, running a race,

Zigging and zooming all over the place,

Upsetting the whale with their earsplitting roar,

Making him swim too close to the shore.

This is the tide, slipping away . . .

And this is the whale lying beached
        in a bay.

"Quick! Off the sand! Back to sea!"
        cried the snail.
"I can't move on land! I'm too big!"
        moaned the whale.

The snail felt helpless and terribly small.
Then, "I've got it!" she cried,
        and started to crawl.

"I must not fail,"
Said the tiny snail.

This is the bell on the school in the bay,

Ringing the children in from their play.

This is the teacher, holding her chalk,

Telling the class, "Sit straight! Don't talk!"

This is the board, as black as soot . . .

And this is the snail with the itchy foot!

"A snail! A snail!"

The teacher turns pale.

"Look!" say the children.

"It's leaving a trail."

This is the trail

Of the tiny snail,

A silvery trail saying . . .

Save the whale

These are the children, running from school,

Fetching the firemen, digging a pool,

Squirting and spraying to keep the whale cool.

This is the tide coming into the bay,

And these are the villagers shouting, "Hooray!"

As the whale and the snail travel safely away . . .

Back to the dock

And the flock on the rock,

Who said, "How time's flown!"

And, "Haven't you grown!"

And the whale and the snail

Told their wonderful tale

Of shimmering ice and coral caves,

And shooting stars and enormous waves,

And of how the snail, so small and frail,

With her looping, curling, silvery trail,

Saved the life of the humpback whale.

Then the humpback whale

Held out his tail

And on crawled snail after snail after snail.

And they sang to the sea as they all set sail

On the tail of the grey-blue humpback whale.

For everyone at Hillhead Primary School, Wick ~ J.D.

First published 2003 by Macmillan Children's Books
This edition published 2018 by Macmillan Children's Books
an imprint of Pan Macmillan
20 New Wharf Road, London N1 9RR
Associated companies throughout the world
www.panmacmillan.com

ISBN: 978-1-5098-7882-6

1 3 5 7 9 8 6 4 2

A CIP catalogue record for this book is available
from the British Library.

Printed in Italy.

©Liam Jackson

A Tiny Snail ... and a Tiny Book!

Before illustrator Axel Scheffler started the artwork for *The Snail and the Whale* he made a little tiny version of the book to help him work out what each page might look like. Here are some of the pages from his mini book:

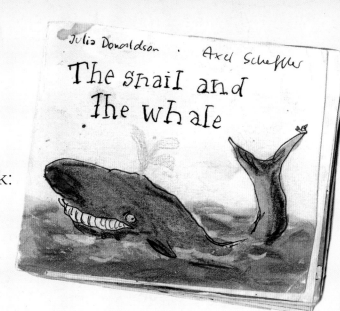

Julia Donaldson · Axel Scheffler

The snail and the whale

This is the story of a tiny snail
And a great big grey-blue hump back whale
This is a rock a black as soot
And this is a snail with a itchy foot

The sea snail slithered all over the rock
And gazed at the sea and the ships in the dock

As she gazed she sniffed and sighed.
"The sea is deep and the world is wide!
How I long to sail!"
Said the tiny snail.

These are the other snails in the flock,
Who all stuck tight to the smooth black rock
And said to the snail with the itchy foot
"Be quiet! "Don't wriggle! Sit still! Stay put!
But the tiny sea snail sighed and sniffed

Then cried "I'll hitch a lift"
This is the trail of the tiny snail
A silvery trail that looped and curled
And said:

Lift wanted
around the world

This is the sea
So wild and free
That carried the whale
And the snail on its tail
For thousands of miles

To icebergs and isles,
To sunsets and rainbows and
faraway isles ... golden sand,

These are the waves ...

on the tail of the whale

But then came the day when the whale lost his way

These are the speed boats, running a race
Zigzag and zooming all over the place
Confusing the whale with their earsplitting voom
Making him swim too close
to the shore

whale bigger!

Can you find similar pictures in the final book?
Have a look to see how much they have changed.